MY FAVORITE DOG

BLOODHOUNDS

by Renata Marie

Kaleidoscope
Minneapolis, MN

BIGFOOT BOOKS

The Quest for Discovery Never Ends

This edition first published in 2022 by Kaleidoscope Publishing, Inc.

*For information regarding permission, write to
Kaleidoscope Publishing, Inc.
6012 Blue Circle Drive
Minnetonka, MN 55343*

*Library of Congress Control Number
2021934889*

*ISBN
978-1-64519-467-5 (library bound)
978-1-64519-475-0 (ebook)*

Printed in the United States of America.

FIND ME IF YOU CAN!

Bigfoot lurks within one of the images in this book. It's up to you to find him!

TABLE OF CONTENTS

Introduction

Hide-and-Sniff!

Trevor weaves through the trees. He jumps over a bush. He has to find a place to hide. A group of pine trees stands to his right. He runs in a circle around a bench before ducking under the branches. A howl like a deep, sad song echoes through the park. *Aaaa-OoooooOooooo!* The hunt has begun.

Trevor sits down. He tucks his legs to his chest and holds his breath. Soon he can hear the sniffs of a nose low to the ground. Then the sound is gone. Trevor takes the chance to peek under the pine branches. A big wrinkly dog head shoves its way into his hiding place and licks his face. "You found me! Good girl, Sally!"

Chapter 1

The Story of Bloodhounds

Horses plod through the trees after a pack of Bloodhounds. Hunters ready their arrows. The dogs sniff in circles and continue their run. A deer is near, and whoever shoots it is the winner. It's one of the most popular games in medieval times. A Bloodhound howls. A deer leaps. An arrow flies. The bishop wins!

Records of hounds with strong noses date back to ancient Mediterranean times, but it wasn't until medieval times that Bloodhounds were developed as **trackers**. The grounds of monasteries in France and England housed packs of Bloodhounds. Even bishops **rode** them in hunting games.

FUN FACT

A Bloodhound has approximately 230 million scent receptors. Humans only have six million. This means Bloodhounds can follow scent trails up to 130 miles (210 kilometers) away.

TRACKING MACHINES

Bloodhounds are known for their strong noses. Their ears and wrinkles help them pick up scents, too. The wrinkles in their skin trap scent **particles**, and when Bloodhounds have their noses to the ground, their big ears sweep up smells into their nostrils! Their strong shoulder and leg muscles help them stick to a scent for miles on end. Bloodhounds really are built for tracking.

A Basset Hound

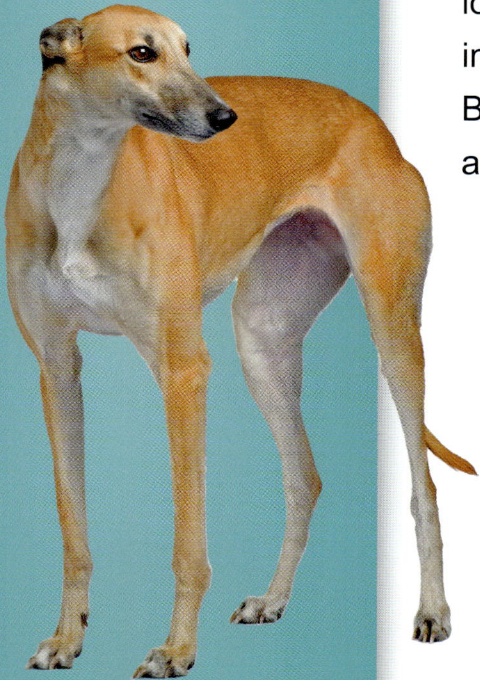
A Greyhound

Bloodhounds like Sally are not the only dogs that were bred to track. Dog breeds are put into groups. Bloodhounds are in the Hound Group. Dogs in the Hound Group were bred to hunt. Some can track by eyesight, others by smell, and some have a lot of **stamina**. Other dogs in the Hound Group include Basset Hounds, Beagles, and Greyhounds.

A Beagle

A Bloodhound and its trainer at a Westminster Kennel Club Dog Show

Bloodhounds are known as sleuthhounds for their ability to find people who are lost or hiding.

After their game of hide-and-seek at the park, Trevor and Sally arrive home. Trevor's dad is already serving Grandpa Max his lunch. Sally is really Grandpa Max's dog. After Sally **retired** from search and rescue work, Trevor's family adopted her. Now she helps them find Grandpa Max when he goes on his morning walk without telling anyone. Grandpa Max has **Alzheimer's**. Sometimes he forgets things, like where he is. Sally always brings him home.

FUN FACT

The first record of Bloodhounds used in organized law enforcement was in England in 1805. A Bloodhound was used to search for poachers and thieves.

Where BLOODHOUNDS come from

Chapter 2

Looking at a Bloodhound

Grandpa Max sits in his recliner. Sally lounges on the couch beside him. Both are asleep. Trevor thinks Grandpa Max would look like Sally if he were a dog. His long face has more wrinkles than Sally's. And she has a lot of wrinkles! Both have skin that hangs a bit loose, and they both have droopy eyes and ears.The matching pair snores. Trevor laughs. *They're perfect for each other,* he thinks.

WRINKLED, WISE KINGS

During medieval times, monks bred hounds so carefully that the dogs became known as "blooded hounds." During that time, royalty usually only married others of royal blood. To be called "blooded" meant Bloodhounds were like royalty in the dog world.

THE BLOODHOUND

MALES

HEIGHT:*
25-27 inches (64-69 cm)

WEIGHT:
90-110 pounds (41-50 kg)

FEMALES

HEIGHT:*
23-25 inches (58-64 cm)

WEIGHT:
80-100 pounds (36-45 kg)

**The height of a dog is measured from the top of the shoulder, not from the top of the head.*

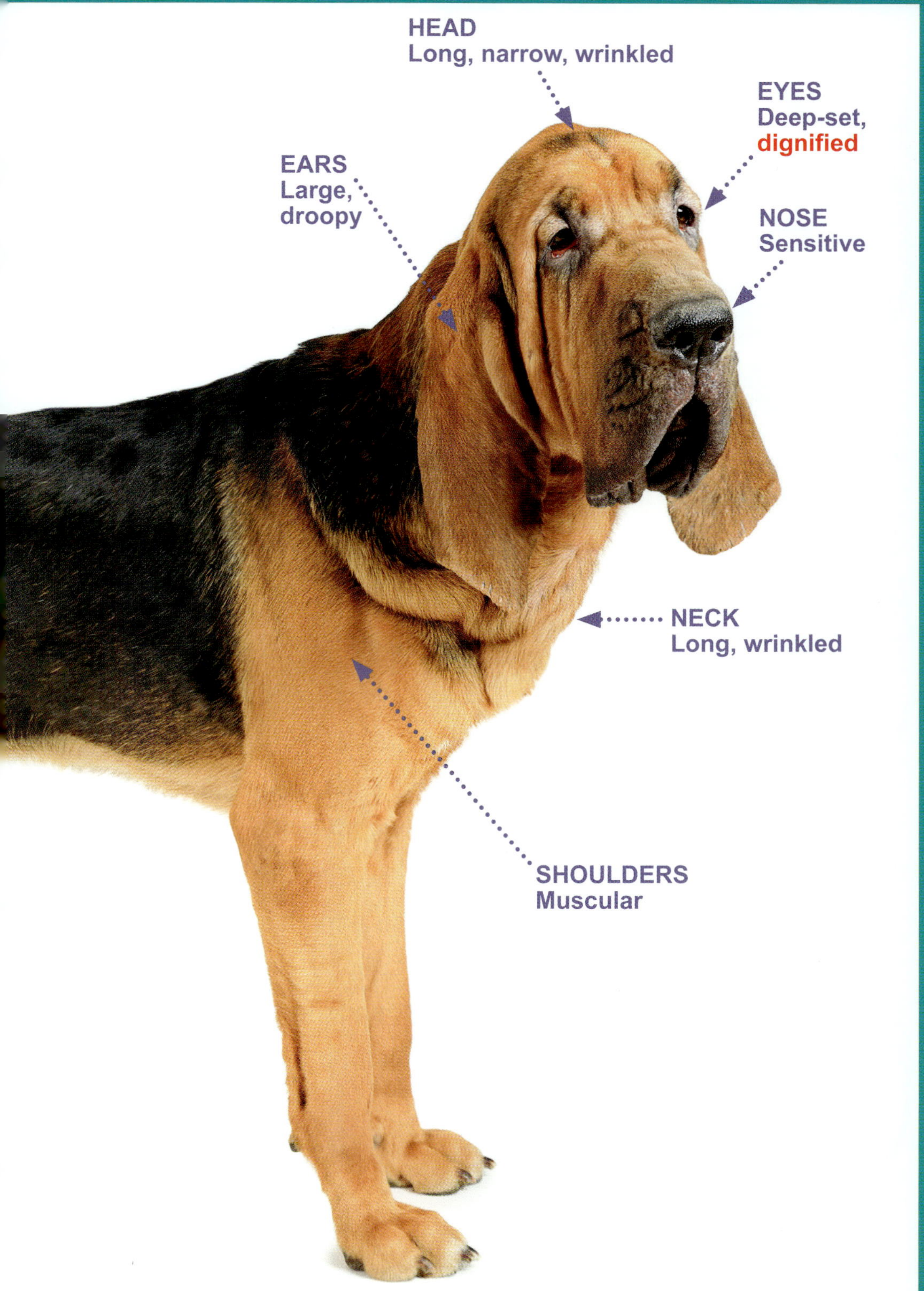
HEAD
Long, narrow, wrinkled
EYES
Deep-set, dignified
EARS
Large, droopy
NOSE
Sensitive
NECK
Long, wrinkled
SHOULDERS
Muscular

A black and tan Bloodhound

A red Bloodhound with white spots

A liver and tan Bloodhound

Bloodhound coats can be many different colors. They can be black and tan, red, and sometimes they can have white spots. They can also be the color of liver. Liver is a red-brown color. Sometimes, liver coats can look pink.

No matter their coat color, Bloodhounds usually look dignified. When Trevor takes Sally to the park, her **gait** is easygoing, but she holds herself with pride. She looks like she owns the park. It's no wonder people have loved Bloodhounds for more than one thousand years.

Bloodhounds have changed very little over time. If you compared ancient Bloodhounds to those today, you couldn't tell them apart!

Chapter 3

Meet a Bloodhound!

After their nap, Grandpa Max wants to take Sally out for an afternoon walk. He likes to take care of her as much as she likes to take care of him. Trevor remembers the day Sally came to live with them. Like other Bloodhounds, Sally was instantly friendly. She loved to play with Trevor, and she always stuck by Grandpa Max's side when they were home. It was like she knew it was her job to keep track of him.

Trevor and his dad join Grandpa Max and Sally on their walk. Trevor's dad holds the leash. Even though they're friendly, Bloodhounds like Sally are strong. They can tug hard on the leash if they catch a scent trail.

Search and rescue dogs begin training when they are still puppies.

A police dog on a scent trail

Bloodhounds can be stubborn and independent. Once they learn **habits**, they stick to them. It's hard to teach old Bloodhounds new tricks. Luckily, Sally was trained well as a search and rescue dog.

FUN FACT

Bloodhounds were bred to track in packs. Search and rescue dogs like Sally often work with other dogs to find missing people. The more noses at work, the more likely the Bloodhounds can find their scent.

What should be a short walk takes an hour. Bloodhounds like Sally love the company of other dogs and people. She stops and says “hi” to the neighbor at the end of the street. She sniffs each dog they pass by. It’s like she has to greet everyone. Trevor sometimes feels like Sally is the queen of the neighborhood.

Chapter 4

Caring for a Bloodhound

While Grandpa Max and Trevor's dad make dinner, Trevor grabs the dog brush. Sally trots over, tail wagging. She sits at his feet and waits expectantly. Brushing Bloodhounds weekly keeps their coats healthy. Bloodhounds like Sally have short fur, but it's thick. She'll shed once or twice each year. That means a lot of brushing for Trevor!

You can also groom Bloodhounds with a rubber grooming mitt. The mitt has little rubber tips instead of bristles.

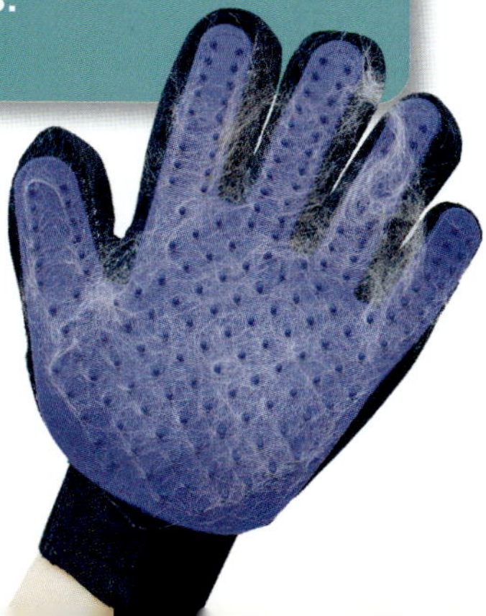

LOTS OF EAR

Bloodhound ears are great at catching sounds, but they also catch dirt, heat, and moisture—the perfect place for germs to grow. To keep Bloodhounds healthy, owners should clean their ears once a day with a clean, wet, warm towel and clean more thoroughly once a week.

After brushing Sally, Trevor bathes her. He uses dog shampoo the **veterinarian** recommended. Bloodhounds need to be bathed regularly or they'll start to smell.

"Dinnertime!" Grandpa Max calls. He's already set out a bowl of dog food for Sally. After playing hide-and-seek and walking, Sally sure is hungry!

It's almost time for bed. While Trevor brushes his teeth, Sally sits at the bathroom door. She knows bedtime means clean teeth for her, too. Trevor uses a toothpaste made for dogs. Human toothpaste would make Sally sick.

Bloodhounds need their nails trimmed regularly.

A finger toothbrush for dogs cleans hard-to-reach areas to keep your pet healthy.

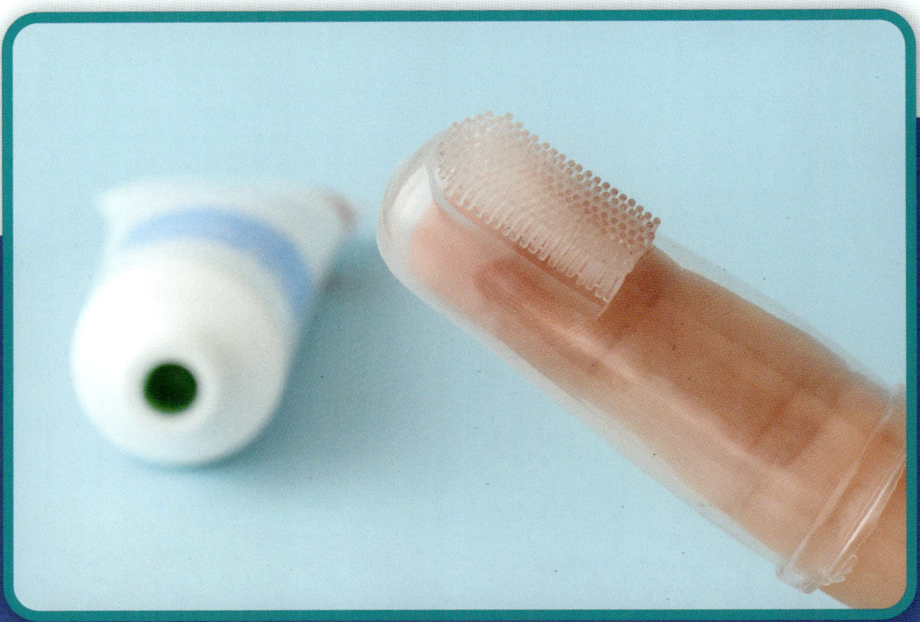

Sally curls up in her dog bed. Trevor pets her head as her eyes start to droop. "Good night, Sally," Trevor says. Sally sleeps in a dog bed by the front door just in case Grandpa Max gets confused when he wakes up. Trevor is so thankful for her good work. It means he gets to live with his grandpa. He thinks Sally is the best dog a kid could ask for!

FUN FACT

Some people believe Bloodhounds are lazy and like to lie around, but Bloodhounds are actually active dogs. They were bred to track for miles. A Bloodhound that doesn't track needs exercise.

BEYOND THE BOOK

After reading the book, it's time to think about what you learned. Try the following exercises to jump-start your ideas.

THINK

FIND OUT MORE. There is so much more to dig up about Bloodhounds. What do you want to learn? Find out more on the American Kennel Club website. Or look for a Bloodhound club in your area. You can meet people who love them as much as you do!

CREATE

ART TIME. Can you draw a Bloodhound? Look up a cute picture and grab some markers and paper. Will your pup have a fancy hairstyle? Will it wear a fun hat? What is its favorite toy or game? Does it have a job? The sky is the limit!

SHARE

THE MORE WHO KNOW. Share what you learned about Bloodhounds. Use your own words to write a paragraph. What are the main ideas of this book? What facts from the book can you use to support those ideas? Share your paragraph with a classmate. Do they have any comments or questions about Bloodhounds?

GROW

HELP OUT! There are dogs near you that need care. Animal shelters can be great places to volunteer and hang out with pups. Contact a shelter near you and find out if you can help. Or can your family donate food or gear to help rescue dogs? Find out why dogs end up in shelters. Is there anything you can do to help them find homes?

RESEARCH NINJA

Visit *www.ninjaresearcher.com/4675* to learn how to take your research skills and book report writing to the next level!

DIGITAL LITERACY TOOLS

Research

SEARCH LIKE A PRO
Learn how to use search engines to find useful websites.

FACT OR FAKE
Discover how you can tell a trusted website from an untrustworthy resource.

TEXT DETECTIVE
Explore how to zero in on the information you need most.

SHOW YOUR WORK
Research responsibly—learn how to cite sources.

DOWNLOADABLE BOOK REPORT FORMS

Write

GET TO THE POINT
Learn how to express your main ideas.

PLAN OF ATTACK
Learn prewriting exercises and create an outline.

Further Resources

BOOKS

Bowman, Chris. *Awesome Dogs: Bloodhounds*. Minnetonka, Minn.: Bellwether Media, Inc., 2020.

Miller, Mirella S. *Helping Dogs: Search and Rescue Dogs on the Job.* Mankato, Minn.: Child's World, 2017.

Rudolph, Jessica. *Bow Wow! Dog Helpers: Search-and-Rescue Dogs.* Minneapolis, Minn.: Bearport Publishing, 2014.

WEBSITES

FACTSURFER

Factsurfer.com gives you a safe, fun way to find more information.

1. Go to www.factsurfer.com.
2. Enter "Bloodhounds" into the search box and click
3. Select your book cover to see a list of related websites.

Glossary

Alzheimer's: a disease where you slowly lose your memories in your elder years.

dignified: having a serious look that is worthy of respect.

gait: the way a person or animal walks.

habit: a behavior an animal or person does over and over again.

monks: a member of a religious community of men who take a vow to the church.

particles: a very tiny piece of something.

retire: to leave a job or sport at the end of a career.

rode: hunting with Bloodhounds or another tracking breed while on horseback is called riding.

stamina: the ability to do something hard for a long time.

tracker: an animal or person who follows a trail to find someone or something. Bloodhounds use their strong noses to track animals and lost people.

veterinarian: a doctor for animals.

Index

PHOTO CREDITS

The images in this book are reproduced through the courtesy of: Erik Lam/Shutterstock Images, cover and p. 1; Maximillian Laschon/Shutterstock Images, p. 1 (paw prints); Kuznetsov Alexey/Shutterstock Images, p. 3; Slatan/Shutterstock Images, p. 5; Anna Tronova/Shutterstock Images, p. 5 (bottom right); mikedabell/iStockphoto, p. 6; Mia Wells/Shutterstock Images, p. 7; Susan Schmitz/Shutterstock Images, p. 8 (Basset Hound); Kuznetsov Alexey/Shutterstock Images, p. 8 (Bloodhound); Eric Isselee/Shutterstock Images, p. 8 (Greyhound); Svetography/Shutterstock Images, p. 8 (Beagle); Debby Wong/Shutterstock Images, p. 9 (top); Kuznetsov Alexey/Shutterstock Images, p. 9 (bottom); X2Photo/iStockphoto, p. 10; Danita Delimont/Shutterstock Images, p. 12; Anna Tronova/Shutterstock Images, p. 13; Lawrey/Shutterstock Images, p. 13, (crown); Kuznetsov Alexey/Shutterstock Images, p. 14-15; camillekphotography/Shutterstock Images, p. 16 (top); claudio.arnese/iStockphoto, p. 16 (middle); Blue Tick Sugar Images/Shutterstock Images, p. 16 (bottom); NSC Photography/Shutterstock Images, p. 17; Ermolaev Alexander/Shutterstock Images, p. 18; Edoma/Shutterstock Images, p. 19 (top); Sidra Monreal Photography/Shutterstock Images, p. 19 (bottom); X2Photo/iStockphoto, p. 20; Edoma /Shutterstock Images, p. 21; Yuliya Alekseeval/Shutterstock Images, p. 22 (left); Erik Lam/Shutterstock Images, p. 22 (right); dageldog /iStockphoto, p. 23; Kuznetsov Alexey/Shutterstock Images, p. 24 (top); Pavel Vinnik/Shutterstock Images, p. 24 (bottom); Goldution/Shutterstock Images, p. 25 (top); Maryia_K/Shutterstock Images, p. 25 (bottom); Kuznetsov Alexey/Shutterstock Images, p. 26-27; Erik Lam/Shutterstock Images, p. 30.

About the Author

Renata Marie is a children's book editor and author. She has also written a young adult novel and flash fiction. Renata loves sharing her stories with her mom's classroom and hanging out with her two overly curious cats and big lap dog, Takoda.